For Tilia and Sylvie for being
so very patient with the tortoise
P.W.

For Glenn and Jonathan
C.C.

THE HARE
AND THE TORTOISE

Retold by Caroline Castle

Illustrated by Peter Weevers

Dial Books for Young Readers

E. P. DUTTON, INC. NEW YORK

Hare got out of bed one morning feeling so fit that he jumped two feet in the air for the fun of it.

"Never was there a faster hare," he said, as he admired himself in the mirror. He did his exercises, brushed his teeth, and set off for his morning run.

The sun was just coming up. Hare took a deep breath and started out at a fast pace. He moved like the wind, jumping hedges and leaping streams. Three times he went around the forest and wasn't at all tired when he finished.

On his way back Hare met Badger who was busy sweeping the path to his house.

"Morning, Badger," said Hare.

"Morning, Hare," said Badger. "Been out running?"

"As I do every morning," said Hare in his superior voice. "I'm *very* fit." And he stood on his hands to prove it. Badger only yawned.

"Show off," Badger said to himself after Hare left.

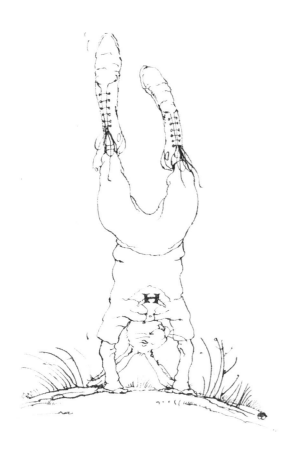

That same morning Tortoise was sitting up in bed working on his book, *Great Tortoises of the World*. He'd been writing it for years, two pages each day. Just as he finished page 1749, he realized he was hungry.

"Oh, I've forgotten breakfast again," said Tortoise. Then he looked out of the window. It was a fine day. "I think I'll go on a picnic," he said.

Tortoise filled a basket with food and two bottles of his favorite lettuce juice.

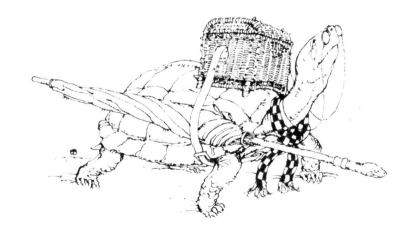

Just as Tortoise had sat down by the river with his book, Hare came along. There was something about Tortoise that really annoyed Hare, but he couldn't figure out what it was. Maybe it was the way Tortoise stayed in bed until lunchtime, or the way he never cared what time it was, or the way he smiled that silly smile as if he knew some wonderful secret.

"Just out of bed, Tortoise?" Hare asked. "You'll never get anyplace lying around reading books all the time."

"Beats running in circles," replied Tortoise. "Where does that get you?"

"Places you'll never see," said Hare. "I'm the fastest hare around."

"That's what you think," mumbled Tortoise. "I'd bet that despite all your speed, even I could beat you in one of your hairbrained races."

Hare laughed so hard that his sides ached and so loudly that Badger and Mole came to see what was going on. "Tortoise has just challenged me to a race," said Hare, still laughing. "ME! The fastest hare in the country."

"Well," said Badger, "why don't you take Tortoise on?"

And so Hare did.

They picked a day for the race.
Badger sold tickets for a penny each.
Mole tried to mark out the track by digging
a line of molehills. But no matter how
hard he tried, he couldn't seem to get them
to come up in the right places.

Frog was in charge of announcing the race. He traveled all over the countryside calling in his loud, hoarse voice: "Attention! Attention! The race between Hare and Tortoise will be on Sunday afternoon at three o'clock. Come early to see all. Tickets one penny each."

When the day arrived, the air buzzed with excitement. Frog was selling balloons: a red one if you rooted for Hare and a green one if you rooted for Tortoise. Squirrel set up a snack-bar tent with tables and chairs outside. Even Fox, who never went to anything, showed up at the last minute.

Of course, Hare was the first runner to arrive for the race. He bounced in and started to warm up on the sidelines, while friends from his running club cheered him on. At last, just moments before the race was about to begin, Tortoise leisurely strolled up. But before going to the starting line, he sat and had some lemonade with Squirrel.

Finally Badger called for the race to start. "On your mark, get set, go!" He dropped his handkerchief and they were off. All the animals waved their balloons, threw up their hats, and cheered and cheered.

Before long, Hare was so far in front that when he looked back Tortoise wasn't even in sight.

Hare started to slow down.

"What a dumb race," he said to some animals sitting on the bank. "It's below me. I'll bet that there's not another hare in the world who would even consider racing Tortoise."

It was a sunny day with a blue sky and Hare decided to take a short rest. Even if he slept all day, Tortoise would never catch up with him.

Hare relaxed as the sweet smell of summer drifted over him. The scents of honeysuckle and rose, lavender and sweet pea lulled him into a deep sleep.

He began to dream. It was the day of the Fastest Hare Race. All the great hares were there: Swiftly, Fast Legs, and Leaper— his heroes. Hare led the race from the beginning and soon was so far in front he had time to look back and see the others way behind.

He came in first, and the crowd's cheer was so loud that he awoke with a start.

But the cheer wasn't for him. When Hare opened his eyes, he saw Tortoise just about to cross the finish line. He jumped up and ran as fast as he could.

Hare was too late. Tortoise had won. "I can't believe it. You beat me!" said Hare, astonished.

"Yes," replied Tortoise. "By a hair's breadth, you could say."

Just another day, thought Tortoise. And he ambled home to write another page of his book.

First published in the United States 1985 by
Dial Books for Young Readers
A Division of E. P. Dutton, Inc.
2 Park Avenue, New York, New York 10016
Published in Great Britain by Hutchinson Children's Books Ltd.

Printed and bound in Great Britain
First edition
US
10 9 8 7 6 5 4 3 2 1

Library of Congress Cataloging in Publication Data
Castle, Caroline.
The hare and the tortoise.
Summary: Relates the events of the famous race
between the boastful hare and the persevering tortoise.
[1. Fables.]   I. Weevers, Peter, ill.   II. Title.
PZ8.2.C36Har   1985   398.2'452   [E]   84-9569
ISBN 0-8037-0138-1

The art consists of watercolor paintings, which are
camera-separated and reproduced in full color.